Little RIDDLERS

Yorkshire

Edited By Allie Jones

First published in Great Britain in 2018 by:

YoungWriters

Young Writers
Remus House
Coltsfoot Drive
Peterborough
PE2 9BF
Telephone: 01733 890066
Website: www.youngwriters.co.uk

SB ISBN 978-1-78896-594-1
Printed and bound in the UK by BookPrintingUK
Website: www.bookprintinguk.com
YB0361MZ

FOREWORD

Dear Reader,

Are you ready to get your thinking caps on to puzzle your way through this wonderful collection?

Young Writers' Little Riddlers competition set out to encourage young writers to create their own riddles. Their answers could be whatever or whoever their imaginations desired; from people to places, animals to objects, food to seasons. Riddles are a great way to further the children's use of poetic expression, including onomatopoeia and similes, as well as encourage them to 'think outside the box' by providing clues without giving the answer away immediately.

All of us here at Young Writers believe in the importance of inspiring young children to produce creative writing, including poetry, and we feel that seeing their own riddles in print will keep that creative spirit burning brightly and proudly.

We hope you enjoy riddling your way through this book as much as we enjoyed reading all the entries.

CONTENTS

Phoebe Mae Bairstow (5)	63
Rita Wright (6)	64
Jessica Cluny (5)	65
Anabella Snowden (5)	66
Hannah Blue Meier (6)	67
Brooke Rose Beddoes (7)	68
Harrison Dalby (5)	69
Will Clements Nauman (6)	70
Ethan Kenneth Taylor (6)	71
Jackson Allen (5)	72
Ben Galdes (5)	73
Riley James Moore (6)	74
Sam Garlick (6)	75
Jack Garlick (6)	76

Ling Bob JI&N School, Pellon

Leyla May Boulton (6)	77
Niamh McNulty (6)	78
Ellouise Brook (6)	79
Rameesha Hussain (7)	80
Caitlin Adams (6)	81
Ruby-Mae Waddington (5) & Maisie Richer (5)	82
Courtney Rockley (6)	83
Aleksander Sedzicki (5) & Bentley Green	84
Scarlett Owens (5), Morsal Hosmani & Lena Lazarz (5)	85
Finley (6) & Shahyaan Amar (6)	86
Elijah Peart (6)	87
Harriet Olivia Royles (5)	88
Alivia Anderson (6)	89
David-Jack George Copley (6) & Sonny Lee	90
Brooklyn Tasker (6)	91
Kain Dyson-Day (5) & Mason Dewhirst (5)	92
Faye Williams (5) & Safoora Younas	93
Lily-Mae Hayden (5)	94

Loxley Primary School, Loxley

Jack Thomas Layton (6)	95
Bella Rose Capper (7)	96
Nancy Mary Bullas (7)	97
Lily-Jade Hall (7)	98
Emily Verey (6)	99
Georgia Mae Smith (6)	100
Jimmy Whittaker (6)	101
Will Barnett (7)	102
Joe Saxton (6)	103
Nathaniel Kidd (6)	104
Liam Roberts (7)	105
Clara Craddock-Jones (6)	106
Xander Elliott (6)	107
Freddie Wright (7)	108
Isobel Allan (6)	109
Dylan Hornby (7)	110
Lois Erin Micklethwaite (7)	111
Finlay Brookes (6)	112
Beth Lily Edwards (7)	113
Victoria Rodgers (6)	114
Keelan West (7)	115
Finlay Priestley (6)	116

North Ormesby Primary Academy, Middlesbrough

Owen Anthony Dryden-Bates (7)	117
Corey Bruce (7)	118
Oluwatamilore Daji (6)	119
Nevaeh Eland (7)	120
Harley Donnelly (7)	121
Edward Blackburn (7)	122
Tianna Woodier (7)	123
Mohamed Elfalal (7)	124
Kaydie Nettelton (6)	125
Olin Lin (6)	126
Darcie Newton (7)	127
Chloe Jones (6)	128
Lacey Wilkinson (6)	129
Zahra Baig (6)	130
Viola D'Arcangelo (7)	131
Layten Spencer (7)	132

Jack Pattison (7) 133
Laavanya Paramalingam (6) 134
Tharun Ahilan (6) 135

Pollington-Balne CE Primary School & Preschool, Pollington

Ava Tyas (7) 136
Lily May Tomlison (7) 137
Samuel John Kealey (7) 138
George Beard (6) 139
Zoë Mae (6) 140
Darcey Bell (6) 141
Finlay Laycock-Brown (6) 142
Zachary Bamforth (7) 143
Edward Arthur Lacy (6) 144
Chance Downs (7) 145
Kian Biddle (7) 146
Lacey Mae Brook (5) 147
Annabel Bamforth (5) 148
Grace Isabelle Davison (6) 149
Penny Scofyald (6) 150

St Mary & St Joseph RC (VA) Primary School, Pocklington

Inigo Blake-James (7) 151
Henry McLaughlin (6) 152
William Roelofs (6) 153
Jessica Baines (7) 154
Natalie Leia Coldbeck (6) 155
Faith Cherry Patricia Bird (6) 156
Aaron Wilce (7) 157
Max Anthony Burton (7) 158
Hannah Foster (6) 159
Martha Haselock (6) 160
Dale Luke Patrick Feehan (6) 161
Lois Hollingsworth (5) 162
Pamella Kapostina (6) 163
Amy Foster (6) 164
Cadan Barnes (6) 165
Lucy Scott (7) 166
Stanley Pardoe (7) 167

Thorngumbald Primary School, Thorngumbald

Miley Isabell Kirby (6) 168
Holly Ellington-Runkee (7) 169
Erica-Kay Watson (6) 170
Demi Leonard (6) 171
Rosie Cox (5) 172
Jack Marks (7) 173
Imogen Ward (6) 174
Charlotte Finer (6) 175

Woodmansey Primary School, Woodmansey

Jack McKenzie Fletcher (6) 176
Annie Hall (5) 177
Rubie Ellen Cook (7) 178
Darcy Bishop (7) 179
Isaac John Clapham Walker (6) 180
James Wilbor (7) 181
Imogen Eden Ward (7) 182
Alex Fratson (5) 183

THE POEMS

My Small, Furry, Cute Pet

I have four sharp claws.
I have a small head.
I can see in the dark.
I'm ginger and white with a small tail.
I eat pellets for dinner and tea.
I'm small and delicate with orange eyes.
I'm bigger than your finger but smaller than your hand.
What am I?

Answer: A hamster.

Millie Rose Dixon (7)

Ainthorpe Primary School, Hull

What Am I?

I am the biggest star in the sky.
I shine brighter than any other star.
Some say I am brighter than a lamp.
In the summer, people love to see me come
out and get their bikini on.
Don't look at me or I will blind you.
I am a big ball of gas.
What am I?

Answer: A big red sun.

Yvie Lambert (7)
Ainthorpe Primary School, Hull

What Am I?

I live with a family.
I don't stay inside all day.
I like to go out and play.
My owners give me a name.
I like to drink water and I like treats.
I can be held when people don't like me.
I am fluffy and a good swimmer.
What am I?

Answer: A dog.

Coral Hand (6)
Ainthorpe Primary School, Hull

What Am I?

I am black and white, I sometimes bite!
I have four legs and they are short.
I live in Madagascar.
I eat lots of healthy carrots every day.
I climb up high in the tall trees.
I have very small black sharp claws.
What am I?

Answer: A lemur.

Emily Waytzman (6)
Ainthorpe Primary School, Hull

Night-Time And Stars

I sleep in the bright, shining day.
I go hunting in the dark, scary night.
I eat trash and spiders.
I live in a burrow underground.
I have very sharp teeth.
I am ginger and orange.
I have a big bushy tail.
What am I?

Answer: A fox.

Brooke Olivia Thornhill (7)
Ainthorpe Primary School, Hull

Super Swing

I mostly live in warm Africa and Asia.
When it is bedtime, I sleep in a canopy.
I swing on tall branches.
People think I only eat bananas, but I eat
nearly everything.
I am usually brown.
I am cheeky.
What am I?

Answer: A monkey.

Quinn Pattison (6)
Ainthorpe Primary School, Hull

What Am I?

I have four corners.
I can be all different colours.
I have six faces and you can put
nappies in me.
You can use me to put toys in.
You can make things out of me.
Usually, you put baby wipes in me.
What am I?

Answer: A box.

Nathan Flinton (7)
Ainthorpe Primary School, Hull

What Am I?

I have a big, round body.
I live in the huge jungle.
Sometimes I roar loudly.
I hunt very quietly so nobody knows
I'm there.
I'm very fierce.
If you stroke me, your hand will be eaten.
What am I?

Answer: A lion.

Joseph Wood (6)
Ainthorpe Primary School, Hull

What Am I?

I live in a cave and I come out at night.
I have two legs.
I hang upside down on a spiky tree.
I eat leaves.
When I get scared, I cuddle up with my mum and dad.
If you frighten me, I will fly away!
What am I?

Answer: A bat.

Maddie Smith (7)
Ainthorpe Primary School, Hull

Helping Other People

I wear a white, clean jacket.
I can help you by making you better.
Sometimes, I wear a tie.
I am always smart.
I can also help people with babies.
You usually find me in a hospital.
What am I?

Answer: A doctor.

Eliza Adams (6)
Ainthorpe Primary School, Hull

What Am I?

I am a sporty person.
I was born in 2011.
I am a boy or a girl.
I don't play rugby.
I score goals.
I don't play boxing.
I don't play golf.
What am I?

Answer: A footballer.

Lennon Wilcock (6)
Ainthorpe Primary School, Hull

What Am I?

I am a season.
I am tricky if you try and catch me.
I am cold, you will need a hat on.
I drop delicate white flakes on you.
I am ice.
If you skid, I will break!
What am I?

Answer: Winter.

Dawson Radmore (7)
Ainthorpe Primary School, Hull

What Am I?

I am fluffy and cute.
A child usually gives me a name.
Sometimes, I sit on a shelf.
I live in a house.
I come in lots of sizes.
I like to snuggle up in bed.
What am I?

Answer: A teddy.

Imogen Skelly (7)
Ainthorpe Primary School, Hull

Lovely Pets

You can get me as a pet.
If you squeeze me, I may bite you.
I love to hop like a kangaroo.
I like to eat carrots.
I sometimes have white fur.
I hop high.
What am I?

Answer: A bunny.

Maria Sadlek (6)
Ainthorpe Primary School, Hull

My Nasty Friend

I live in the jungle.
People have me as a teddy.
I hunt for my prey.
I have a fierce roar.
I have orange and black fur.
I am king of the jungle.
What am I?

Answer: A lion.

Leo King (7)
Ainthorpe Primary School, Hull

What Am I?

Lots of people love me.
I come in different styles.
People often give me a name.
I will make you better.
I sit on a shelf.
I am fluffy.
What am I?

Answer: A teddy.

Eva Pattrick (6)

Ainthorpe Primary School, Hull

What Am I?

If you smell me, you will sneeze!
I am colourful.
I am pretty.
Sometimes people give me as a present.
I look beautiful.
I smell good.
What am I?

Answer: A flower.

Ayssal Uzbek (6)
Ainthorpe Primary School, Hull

What Am I?

I am delicious.
I am skinny.
So easy to cook.
What am I?

Answer: A sausage.

James Vessey (6)
Ainthorpe Primary School, Hull

A Twisted Tale

There are three of us.
We are brown and furry.
Someone called Goldilocks came to our house.
We eat porridge.
We walked in a forest.
There is a big one of us.
There is a medium one of us.
There is a little one of us.
Who are we?

Answer: The Three Bears.

Flossie Boyes (5)
Brandesburton Primary School, Brandesburton

A Twisted Tale

We are pink and a wolf tries to eat us.
We are good at building houses.
We wear dungarees.
One house was made out of straw.
The second house was made out of sticks.
The third house was made out of bricks.
Who are we?

Answer: The Three Little Pigs.

Reuben C (5)
Brandesburton Primary School, Brandesburton

A Twisted Tale

I have long hair, it has flowers in it.
I have a purple dress, but I have no shoes.
I have a wicked stepmother.
I escaped from my tower.
I hit a man with a frying pan.
I would like to see the flowing lights.
Who am I?

Answer: Rapunzel.

Pippa Crawforth (5)

Brandesburton Primary School, Brandesburton

A Twisted Tale

I walked down the path in the woods.
I have a red cape.
I have a basket.
My grandma got eaten by the big bad wolf.
I have red shoes.
The woodcutter saved me by killing the Big Bad Wolf.
Who am I?

Answer: Little Red Riding Hood.

Phoebe Montgomery (5)
Brandesburton Primary School, Brandesburton

A Twisted Tale

I live in a castle with patterns all around.
Around my castle is trees.
I live in a castle and somebody else lives in my castle.
I am furry.
I have two horns.
I fell in love with a beautiful woman.
Who am I?

Answer: *The Beast.*

Thomas A (5)
Brandesburton Primary School, Brandesburton

A Twisted Tale

I went to a castle in the sky.
I sold my cow.
I met a giant.
I took a golden chicken who laid a golden egg.
I climbed up a beanstalk.
I threw the magic beans out of a window.
Who am I?

Answer: Jack (Jack and the Beanstalk).

Luke H (5)
Brandesburton Primary School, Brandesburton

A Twisted Tale

I got made in an oven.
I run away from people.
I have sweeties on me and I also have chocolate on me.
I am coloured brown.
I smell of ginger and I have a red smile.
I rode on a fox.
Who am I?

Answer: *The Gingerbread Man.*

Sophia J (6)
Brandesburton Primary School, Brandesburton

A Twisted Tale

I have two nasty, wicked sisters and a weird stepmother.
I have a nice fairy godmother.
My fairy godmother let me go to the ball.
My shoe fell off as I ran down the steps.
I have a pink dress.
Who am I?

Answer: Cinderella.

Annabelle Lucy Crook (5)
Brandesburton Primary School, Brandesburton

A Twisted Tale

There are three of us.
We build houses.
We are smart.
We tricked the wolf.
We have curly pink tails.
We are clever.
We got the wolf on the bottom of the fire.
Who are we?

Answer: *The Three Little Pigs.*

James Copeland (6)
Brandesburton Primary School, Brandesburton

A Twisted Tale

I smell nice and I smell of ginger.
I am cooked in the oven.
I am decorated with sweets.
Many people try to catch me.
I climb on the fox's back.
I get eaten.
Who am I?

Answer: The Gingerbread Man.

Maisie G (6)
Brandesburton Primary School, Brandesburton

A Twisted Tale

I was made in an oven.
I escaped from an old woman and old man.
I smell of ginger.
I rode on an orange fox.
Two farm animals chased me.
I have buttons.
Who am I?

Answer: The Gingerbread Man.

Charles A (6)
Brandesburton Primary School, Brandesburton

A Twisted Tale

There are three of us.
One of us made a stick house.
We are pink and black.
We are good at building houses.
We have ears.
A wolf chased to get us.
Who are we?

Answer: *The Three Little Pigs.*

Belle F (5)
Brandesburton Primary School, Brandesburton

A Twisted Tale

I have a wicked stepmum.
My stepmum poisoned me.
I was saved by little people.
I was put in a glass box.
I slept in it.
A prince came and kissed me.
Who am I?

Answer: Snow White.

Lacey T (5)
Brandesburton Primary School, Brandesburton

A Twisted Tale

I go in the woods.
I trick people.
I have big ears for listening.
I have big teeth for eating.
I like dressing up as Granny.
I'm grey and fluffy.
Who am I?

Answer: The wolf.

Bella Louise Stevenson (5)
Brandesburton Primary School, Brandesburton

A Twisted Tale

I was cooked in an oven.
I have chocolate chips for my eyes.
I run fast.
I escaped from a house.
I hopped on a fox.
I was eaten.
Who am I?

Answer: The Gingerbread Man.

Josie Evans (5)
Brandesburton Primary School, Brandesburton

A Twisted Tale

I came through a window.
I have a red feather in my hat.
I have a green jacket.
I can fly in the sky.
I don't like Captain Hook.
Who am I?

Answer: Peter Pan.

Lachlan C (6)
Brandesburton Primary School, Brandesburton

A Twisted Tale

I met a wolf in the forest.
I went to grandma's house.
I had a basket with me.
I was eaten.
I was saved.
Who am I?

Answer: Little Red Riding Hood.

Lucy D (5)
Brandesburton Primary School, Brandesburton

A Twisted Tale

I got made in a oven.
I am ginger.
I got baked.
I escaped from a man.
I can be decorated.
I can be eaten.
Who am I?

Answer: The Gingerbread Man.

Arthur Douglas (5)
Brandesburton Primary School, Brandesburton

A Twisted Tale

We have cute tails.
We built houses.
The wolf died in our houses
We set fire to the wolf.
We tricked the wolf.
Who are we?

Answer: Three Little Pigs.

Rosie C (6)
Brandesburton Primary School, Brandesburton

A Twisted Tale

I have long hair.
I have a wicked mother.
I like looking at the stars.
I was locked in a castle.
I have a purple dress.
Who am I?

Answer: Rapunzel.

Nancy Douglas (5)
Brandesburton Primary School, Brandesburton

A Twisted Tale

We are pink.
We made houses.
We don't like the wolf.
We used sticks, straw and bricks to build
our house.
Who are we?

Answer: *Three Little Pigs.*

Oliver W (5)
Brandesburton Primary School, Brandesburton

A Twisted Tale

I like eating animals.
I am brown.
My nose is black.
I chased Little Red Riding Hood.
I ate Grandma.
Who am I?

Answer: The Big Bad Wolf.

James K (6)
Brandesburton Primary School, Brandesburton

A Twisted Tale

I smell good.
I was cooked in an oven.
I have buttons.
I can run very fast.
I got eaten by a fox.
Who am I?

Answer: The Gingerbread Man.

Charlie Pardoe (6)
Brandesburton Primary School, Brandesburton

A Twisted Tale

I go in the woods.
I have brown hair.
I have a yellow basket.
I have a grandma.
I got eaten.
Who am I?

Answer: *Little Red Riding Hood.*

Olivia W (5)

Brandesburton Primary School, Brandesburton

A Twisted Tale

I am in the oven.
I jump up to the window.
My eyes are raisins.
Who am I?

Answer: The Gingerbread Man.

Leo Shipley (5)

Brandesburton Primary School, Brandesburton

A Twisted Tale

I can fly.
I live with the lost boys.
I am green
I am not scary.
Who am I?

Answer: Peter Pan.

Liam C (6)
Brandesburton Primary School, Brandesburton

Fabulous Fantastic Books

I wrote big books.
I was an old man when I died.
I wrote storybooks for children.
I am a famous writer.
I wrote my books at the bottom of my beautiful garden in my brown wooden shed.
I wrote 'The BFG', 'James and the Giant Peach' and 'The Witches'.
Who am I?

Answer: Roald Dahl.

Elena Hooper (7)
Cowling Community Primary School, Cowling

Carnivores

I can live in a house.
I am many different colours.
I have four medium legs.
I like going outside when it's warm.
I have claws as sharp as a sword.
I like to catch things when I go outside.
My favourite thing to catch is mice.
What am I?

Answer: A cat.

Alice Elizabeth Rogerson (7)
Cowling Community Primary School, Cowling

All About Me

I have four legs.
I have sharp teeth.
I eat meat. ·
I have red eyes.
I have sharp claws.
I am grey and I go to hunting in the night.
I am bigger than your feet.
But smaller than the whole body.
I howl in the night.
What am I?

Answer: A werewolf.

James McGill (7)
Cowling Community Primary School, Cowling

Fashion

I am fashionable.

I like to wear beautiful clothes.

I have lots of jobs but I don't do them all.

I am famous because I am a doll.

I have blonde hair and it's long.

I have a huge wardrobe.

I am friends with Ken.

Who am I?

Answer: Barbie.

Evie Rose Lawson (6)

Cowling Community Primary School, Cowling

Under The Sea

I come in many different colours.
I live under the blue sea, but sometimes in a pond or lake.
I come in different shapes and sizes.
I have a floppy tail.
I blow bubbles out of my mouth.
I live in a tank when I'm a pet.
What am I?

Answer: A fish.

Daniel Luke Ashby (7)
Cowling Community Primary School, Cowling

Super Engine

I can come in different colours and sizes.
I have black wheels.
You need to put oil in me or I won't go.
You can ride on me.
I am fast.
I am a vehicle.
I go on mud tracks, but don't go on deep, deep mud.
What am I?

Answer: A motorbike.

Freddie Hay (6)
Cowling Community Primary School, Cowling

Herbivore

I have a long mane flowing down.
I have a long hairy tail.
I have four legs and my legs are really bendy.
I have a short neck.
I drink water and I eat hay.
You can ride me anywhere.
I sleep in my cosy stable.
What am I?

Answer: A horse.

Abby Emmott (6)
Cowling Community Primary School, Cowling

Pink

I have a yellow beak.
I have bumpy webbed feet.
Lots of people see me at the zoo, but I am not always at the zoo.
Sometimes I am at the farm.
I am a bird.
I am bright pink.
Shrimps give me my colour.
What am I?

Answer: A flamingo.

Lavinia Wilkinson (5)
Cowling Community Primary School, Cowling

Seaside

You can decorate me with shells.
You can make me out of sand.
You can put a flag on me.
You can make me at the seaside.
You can give me a flag and a moat.
You can make me with a bucket and spade.
What am I?

Answer: A sandcastle.

Cooper John Hall (6)
Cowling Community Primary School, Cowling

Fantastic Books

I am an author of super books.
I died a long time ago, but I am still very famous.
Some of my books are now films.
I am a male.
I wrote chapter books.
I wrote 'BFG' and 'Matilda'.
Who am I?

Answer: Roald Dahl.

Connie Parkin (7)
Cowling Community Primary School, Cowling

Hunting

I hunt animals.
I eat dead animals.
I am bigger than your head, but smaller than your body!
I have a bushy tail.
I am nocturnal.
I am dark red.
I am the main character in Roald Dahl's books.
Who am I?

Answer: A fox.

Holly Elizabeth Jackson (6)
Cowling Community Primary School, Cowling

Night Animals

It lives in the wild.
It eats meat.
Sometimes, it hunts for food at night.
You don't see one very often.
It comes out at night.
It has a big bushy tail.
It lives in a den.
What is it?

Answer: A fox.

Jacob Tierney (6)
Cowling Community Primary School, Cowling

Track Sport

I have big windows.
I come in different colours.
I get driven by someone.
I am a form of transport.
I have four tyres.
I have windscreen wipers and an engine.
I begin with a C.
What am I?

Answer: A car.

Sam Lightfoot (6)
Cowling Community Primary School, Cowling

Time To Bake

Sometimes I have sprinkles.
I sometimes have gummies.
I sometimes have Skittles.
I sometimes have jam in the middle of me.
You can put candles on me when it is somebody's birthday.
What am I?

Answer: A cake.

Maisey Burden (6)
Cowling Community Primary School, Cowling

Sea Life

I am very big.
I eat whales and little fish.
I have two medium fins.
I have very sharp teeth.
I am dark blue.
I enjoy swimming in the glooming sea.
People are scared of me.
What am I?

Answer: A shark.

Alfie Jackson (6)
Cowling Community Primary School, Cowling

Summer

You can eat it.
It's usually eaten in the summer.
It is cold.
It is a treat.
You can get it from the shops.
You can have sprinkles.
You can eat it from a cone.
What is it?

Answer: Ice cream.

Chloe Christy (5)
Cowling Community Primary School, Cowling

Sweet Tooth

I taste yummy.

I can melt when you don't put me in the fridge.

I am wrapped in foil.

I am made of milk.

I can be black, brown or white.

You can eat me anytime.

What am I?

Answer: Chocolate.

Elsie Howe (6)

Cowling Community Primary School, Cowling

Growing Up

I'm small, but I grow every day.
I drink milk.
I don't go to school yet, but I learn every day.
I suck my thumb.
I can't talk yet.
I wear nappies.
Who am I?

Answer: A baby.

Scarlett Grace Wearmouth (6)
Cowling Community Primary School, Cowling

Paddling

I swim in the water.
I fly in the sky.
I have a beak.
I have some brown and white skinny feathers.
I have a loud quack.
I drink water from my river.
What am I?

Answer: A duck.

Phoebe Mae Bairstow (5)
Cowling Community Primary School, Cowling

Barking Mad

I like to walk and run.
I have four legs.
I have ears.
I have fur.
I wear a collar.
I have a bed.
I bark when someone comes in my house.
What am I?

Answer: A dog.

Rita Wright (6)
Cowling Community Primary School, Cowling

Bells Ring

It can go on the road.
You can sit on it.
It lives in the garage.
You can go on it to the park.
You can stand up on it.
It has two wheels.
What is it?

Answer: A bike.

Jessica Cluny (5)
Cowling Community Primary School, Cowling

My Riddle

It is very tall.
It has a door and a window.
It has a flag.
It is on the beach.
It has a moat.
It is built with buckets and spades.
What is it?

Answer: A sandcastle.

Anabella Snowden (5)
Cowling Community Primary School, Cowling

Yummy

I am brown or white.
I am delicious and yummy.
I can be crunchy.
I am smooth.
I melt in your mouth.
You can make Easter Eggs out of me.
What am I?

Answer: Chocolate.

Hannah Blue Meier (6)
Cowling Community Primary School, Cowling

Magic World

I have two shiny wings.
Sometimes, I am in movies.
I have glitter on me.
I make rainbows.
I have a horn on my forehead.
I'm magic.
What am I?

Answer: A unicorn.

Brooke Rose Beddoes (7)
Cowling Community Primary School, Cowling

Jungle Fun

It has legs.
It eats other animals.
It is big.
It can run fast.
It lives in a hot place.
It lives in Africa.
It has a big mane.
What is it?

Answer: A lion.

Harrison Dalby (5)
Cowling Community Primary School, Cowling

Jaws

I swim.
I have sharp teeth.
I am green.
I lay eggs and then I bury them.
I have a long jaw.
I have scales on my back.
What am I?

Answer: A crocodile.

Will Clements Nauman (6)
Cowling Community Primary School, Cowling

Pets

I have fur.
I can be big or small.
I eat and drink water.
I get treats if I'm good.
I love to walk and run.
I bark.
What am I?

Answer: A dog.

Ethan Kenneth Taylor (6)
Cowling Community Primary School, Cowling

In The Sky

It flies.
It has an engine.
It's got lots of lights.
It's got no windows.
Aliens live in it.
What is it?

Answer: A UFO.

Jackson Allen (5)
Cowling Community Primary School, Cowling

Striking

It is a predator.
It lives in the sea.
It eats dead whales.
It eats fish.
It has a fin.
What is it?

Answer: A shark.

Ben Galdes (5)
Cowling Community Primary School, Cowling

Sea Creature

You can eat it.
It is red.
It eats fish.
It has a sharp tail.
It has two sharp claws.
What is it?

Answer: A lobster.

Riley James Moore (6)
Cowling Community Primary School, Cowling

Seaside Fun

I am made of sand.
You can make me with a bucket.
I have a moat.
The sand has to be wet.
What am I?

Answer: A sandcastle.

Sam Garlick (6)
Cowling Community Primary School, Cowling

Predator Attack

It is grey.
It eats fish.
It is a predator.
It has one sharp fin.
What is it?

Answer: A shark.

Jack Garlick (6)
Cowling Community Primary School, Cowling

Tu-Whit Tu-Whoo

I have two big yellow eyes.
I can see in the dark, but I don't eat carrots.
I can see behind me when I am facing
forwards.
If you go to the woods at night, you might
hear me tu-whit tu-whoo!
What am I?

Answer: An owl.

Leyla May Boulton (6)
Ling Bob JI&N School, Pellon

Tall Story

I have a big long neck.
I roam the African plains.
I eat leaves from tall trees.
I have a fluffy Mohawk down my neck
I have brown squares on my skin.
My legs are long and skinny.
What am I?

Answer: A giraffe.

Niamh McNulty (6)
Ling Bob JI&N School, Pellon

Noisy

All rock stars love me because I'm cool.
My body is round, but I'm long.
I need the strings to work.
If I am not plugged in, I will work,
But I will not be as loud.
What am I?

Answer: A guitar.

Ellouise Brook (6)
Ling Bob JI&N School, Pellon

Let's Have Some Milkshake

I walk on four legs.
I make a moo sound.
I sleep at night-time.
I am black and white.
I am as big as a bull.
I live on the farm.
I don't have any fur.
What am I?

Answer: A cow.

Rameesha Hussain (7)

Ling Bob JI&N School, Pellon

Fruity Veg

I start green and turn red.
I am fruit, not a vegetable.
I can be different sizes.
I grow on a plant.
You can put me in a sandwich or a salad.
What am I?

Answer: A tomato.

Caitlin Adams (6)
Ling Bob JI&N School, Pellon

What Is It?

This animal always swims.
It eats fish.
It is black and white with webbed feet.
This animal likes to catch fish.
It can wiggle its tail.
What is it?

Answer: A penguin.

Ruby-Mae Waddington (5) & Maisie Richer (5)
Ling Bob JI&N School, Pellon

Hunt

Pirates hunt for me.
I live in a box.
I am hidden away.
I am very shiny.
I am coloured gold and silver.
I am hunted for.
What am I?

Answer: Treasure.

Courtney Rockley (6)
Ling Bob JI&N School, Pellon

What Is It?

This animal can be a pet.
It has fur.
It can bark.
It doesn't like cats.
It likes to play with balls.
What is it?

Answer: A dog.

Aleksander Sedzicki (5) & Bentley Green
Ling Bob JI&N School, Pellon

What Is It?

This animal can run fast.
It has got lots of fur.
It's got four legs.
It has a wet, shiny nose.
What is it?

Answer: A dog

Scarlett Owens (5), Morsal Hosmani & Lena Lazarz (5)
Ling Bob JI&N School, Pellon

What Am I?

This animal has a tongue.
It has no legs.
It lives in the jungle.
It sheds its skin.
What is it?

Answer: A snake.

Finley (6) & Shahyaan Amar (6)
Ling Bob JI&N School, Pellon

Juicy Pip

I am a sphere.
I grow on a plant.
You can put me in a salad.
I am juicy.
I am red.
What am I?

Answer: A tomato.

Elijah Peart (6)
Ling Bob JI&N School, Pellon

What Is It?

This animal runs fast.
It can wag its tail.
It has food.
It can bark.
It can climb.
What is it?

Answer: A dog.

Harriet Olivia Royles (5)
Ling Bob JI&N School, Pellon

Stripes

I look like a horse.
I eat grass.
I can live in a zoo.
I have black and white stripes.
What am I?

Answer: A zebra.

Alivia Anderson (6)
Ling Bob JI&N School, Pellon

What Is It?

This animal has a big fin.
It is not a pet
It lives in the sea.
It has sharp teeth.
What is it?

Answer: A shark

David-Jack George Copley (6) & Sonny Lee

Ling Bob JI&N School, Pellon

Hunter

I have sharp teeth.
I have sharp claws.
I am orange and black.
I like to roar.
What am I?

Answer: A tiger.

Brooklyn Tasker (6)
Ling Bob JI&N School, Pellon

What Is It?

This animal has fast legs.
It howls.
It lives in parks.
It is grey.
What is it?

Answer: A fox.

Kain Dyson-Day (5) & Mason Dewhirst (5)
Ling Bob JI&N School, Pellon

What Is It?

This animal has four legs.
It has a tail
It has fur.
It can bark.
What is it?

Answer: A dog.

Faye Williams (5) & Safoora Younas
Ling Bob JI&N School, Pellon

What Is It?

This animal has fur.
It can run fast.
It can bark and has sharp teeth.
What is it?

Answer: A dog.

Lily-Mae Hayden (5)
Ling Bob JI&N School, Pellon

Who Am I?

I visit you once a year and I hope to bring joy and cheer.

I will deliver toys to all good girls and boys.

You must remember to be fast asleep and try your best not to peep.

Please don't forget to leave a mince pie and my reindeer need carrots for their eyes.

Down the chimney, I will fall and bring presents in my sack for you all.

In the morning, rush to check under the tree and hope that you will squeal with glee to see all the presents to you from me.

Who am I?

Answer: Father Christmas.

Jack Thomas Layton (6)
Loxley Primary School, Loxley

The Mystical Creature

There is a creature that lives under my bed.
I wanted to call him Jojo, but his name
is Fred.
His horn is sparkly and his mane is swishy,
His eyes are magical, but his breath
smells fishy!
He prances around my bedroom with his
glitter hooves,
We dance around together and I have the
best dance moves!
What is he?

Answer: A unicorn.

Bella Rose Capper (7)
Loxley Primary School, Loxley

Magic Mania

I have four hooves and a beautiful mane.
I could live in your dream world far, far
away or in a stable eating some hay.
I have sparkly eyes.
I am fluffy and sparkly.
I can gallop or fly.
I have a colourful thing on the top of my
head.
This may give you a clue, but I hope not yet!
What am I?

Answer: A unicorn.

Nancy Mary Bullas (7)
Loxley Primary School, Loxley

Guess Me

I am made with an egg,
But I haven't got any legs.
I can be as long as a pole,
But I can also fit in a hole.
I can be kept as a pet,
But I eat small animals if I'm let.
Lots of different colours, I can be.
I slither when things come near me.
What am I?

Answer: A snake.

Lily-Jade Hall (7)
Loxley Primary School, Loxley

Down On The Farm

I can fly.
I am red.
I can make drumsticks, but I can't play the drums.
I live in a flock and have feathers.
I live on a farm and have a beak.
I'm not very calm.
My wings are spicy.
I make a nice stock.
What am I?

Answer: A chicken.

Emily Verey (6)
Loxley Primary School, Loxley

What Am I?

I weigh between 75kg and 135kg.
There are only one thousand of us left.
I don't hibernate.
I live in China or zoos.
I am black and white.
I eat bamboo and leaves.
We have lived on Earth for two to three million years.
What am I?

Answer: A panda.

Georgia Mae Smith (6)
Loxley Primary School, Loxley

Sting

I am in the spider family.
I live in all continents except for Antarctica.
I was around 430 million years ago.
There are 1750 different species of me.
I have a long curly tail.
Don't step on me in the desert!
What am I?

Answer: A scorpion.

Jimmy Whittaker (6)
Loxley Primary School, Loxley

Fur-Ocious!

I'm the biggest of my kind, that's right.
I hunt alone and only at night.
For camouflage, my fur is striped.
If I'm really rare, my fur is white.
Humans hunt me for my fur.
I live all over Asia.
What am I?

Answer: A tiger.

Will Barnett (7)
Loxley Primary School, Loxley

The Little Creature

I am a tiny creature with sharp claws and pointy hairs.
I love to roam at night.
I love to look for a tiny bit of food.
I have lots of long pointy spikes and if you give me a pat, I will curl up in a ball.
What am I?

Answer: A hedgehog.

Joe Saxton (6)
Loxley Primary School, Loxley

Scary

I am dark green,
I thump across the land.
Hunting for my meat.
I have bone-crunching teeth.
I am as tall and as long as a
double-decker bus.
I have enormous powerful legs but tiny
arms.
What am I?

Answer: A T-rex.

Nathaniel Kidd (6)
Loxley Primary School, Loxley

Sneaky And Slithery

I am light green and dark green.
I wind from side to side.
I have no legs.
I like to flick out my tongue.
My mouth is very small, but it can open very wide.
My skin is like an orange.
What am I?

Answer: A snake.

Liam Roberts (7)
Loxley Primary School, Loxley

My Best Friend

I love to play with a ball.
I catch it with my mouth every time.
With my four legs I run, then I yelp and
I bark.
When I'm happy, I waggle my tail!
What am I?

Answer: A dog.

Clara Craddock-Jones (6)
Loxley Primary School, Loxley

Strong

I am strong.
My fur is black and my eyes are brown.
I live on the ground.
I am a mammal.
I am the biggest primate.
I live in the rainforest.
What am I?

Answer: A gorilla.

Xander Elliott (6)
Loxley Primary School, Loxley

Land Of Ice And Snow

I love swimming.
My favourite food is fish.
We live in Antarctica.
I have wings but I can't fly.
I am black and white.
I am an emperor.
What am I?

Answer: A penguin.

Freddie Wright (7)
Loxley Primary School, Loxley

Can You Spot What I Am?

Some live in hot places, some live in cold places.
I have lots of spots.
I have a group called a leap.
Sometimes, I hunt.
I'm a big cat.
What am I?

Answer: A leopard.

Isobel Allan (6)
Loxley Primary School, Loxley

The Big Cat

I am a big cat that runs very fast,
so, in a race, I'm never last.
I have spotty fur,
I eat meat.
In Africa, you'll find my feet.
What am I?

Answer: A cheetah.

Dylan Hornby (7)
Loxley Primary School, Loxley

What Is It?

I have one.
You have one.
We all have one.
I will use yours more than mine.
You answer to it.
You will have it all your life.
What is it?

Answer: Your name.

Lois Erin Micklethwaite (7)
Loxley Primary School, Loxley

Bird Spotting

I am a bird.
I am nocturnal and hunt at night.
I can be snowy.
In Harry Potter, my name is Hedwig.
I am a mascot for SWFC.
What am I?

Answer: An owl.

Finlay Brookes (6)
Loxley Primary School, Loxley

Purr

We all look different.
We are pets.
We have fur.
Lots of people own us.
Some of us are fluffy,
We are animals.
What are we?

Answer: Cats.

Beth Lily Edwards (7)
Loxley Primary School, Loxley

What Am I?

I am fluffy.
I am soft.
I have a tail.
I have paws.
I have whiskers.
I am black and white.
What am I?

Answer: A cat.

Victoria Rodgers (6)
Loxley Primary School, Loxley

Afraid

I have hairy long legs.
I like to spin webs.
I have lots of eyes,
So I can see flies.
What am I?

Answer: A spider.

Keelan West (7)
Loxley Primary School, Loxley

Fire Wars

I can be red.
I can be green.
I breathe fire.
I can be heard but not seen.
What am I?

Answer: A dragon.

Finlay Priestley (6)
Loxley Primary School, Loxley

A Woodland Animal

I have a group that is called a leash.
I have whiskers.
My colour can be red, orange and grey.
I live in woodland areas.
I am dangerous to animals because I am a carnivore.
I am a member of the dog family.
What am I?

Answer: A fox.

Owen Anthony Dryden-Bates (7)
North Ormesby Primary Academy, Middlesbrough

A Woodland Animal

I peck holes in trees to find insects.
I am an omnivore.
I can peck twenty times per second.
I look like a songbird.
I live in forests all over the world.
I have a red, white and black face.
What am I?

Answer: A woodpecker.

Corey Bruce (7)
North Ormesby Primary Academy, Middlesbrough

Woodland Animal

I'm an insect.
My life cycle is made of four parts.
I attach my eggs to leaves with special glue.
I am a herbivore.
I can live as a grown-up between a week
and a year.
What am I?

Answer: A butterfly.

Oluwatamilore Daji (6)
North Ormesby Primary Academy, Middlesbrough

Woodland Animal

A group of us is called a skulk or leash.
I have whiskers to help me navigate.
I have a long nose.
We can be grey, orange or white.
I am a carnivore.
I am nocturnal.
What am I?

Answer: A fox.

Nevaeh Eland (7)
North Ormesby Primary Academy, Middlesbrough

A Woodland Animal

I am spiky.
I like to eat slugs.
I hibernate in the winter.
I am nocturnal.
I live in gardens and bushes.
I curl up into a ball when I'm scared.
What am I?

Answer: A hedgehog.

Harley Donnelly (7)
North Ormesby Primary Academy, Middlesbrough

A Woodland Animal

I like to eat nuts and fruit.
I like to climb trees.
I can be grey or red.
I have big eyes.
I store food in my cheeks.
I live in parks and woods.
What am I?

Answer: A squirrel.

Edward Blackburn (7)

North Ormesby Primary Academy, Middlesbrough

A Woodland Animal

I have short brown hair.
I hibernate in the winter.
I have a fluffy tail and small black eyes.
I like to eat hazelnuts.
I belong to the rodent family.
What am I?

Answer: A dormouse.

Tianna Woodier (7)
North Ormesby Primary Academy, Middlesbrough

A Woodland Animal

I have grey fur all over me.
I have long ears.
I have whiskers.
I live in a burrow.
I eat grass.
I have babies that are called kittens or a kit.
What am I?

Answer: A rabbit.

Mohamed Elfalal (7)
North Ormesby Primary Academy, Middlesbrough

A Woodland Animal

I am an omnivore.
My feathers are waterproof.
I have webbed feet.
I waddle instead of walk.
I cannot feel the cold.
My mouth is called a bill.
What am I?

Answer: A duck.

Kaydie Nettelton (6)
North Ormesby Primary Academy, Middlesbrough

Woodland Animal

I have whiskers.
I can be orange, red or grey.
I can hear up to forty yards away.
I can see at night.
My pupils are vertical.
I am a carnivore.
What am I?

Answer: A fox.

Olin Lin (6)
North Ormesby Primary Academy, Middlesbrough

Woodland Animal

I am orange.
I have big sharp teeth.
I eat other animals.
I live in woods and forest.
I come out at night.
I have four legs and a brushy tail.
What am I?

Answer: A fox.

Darcie Newton (7)
North Ormesby Primary Academy, Middlesbrough

Woodland Animal

I have long ears.
I have fur.
I live in burrows.
I have babies that are called kittens.
I have whiskers.
I live in a group called a colony.
What am I?

Answer: A rabbit.

Chloe Jones (6)

North Ormesby Primary Academy, Middlesbrough

Woodland Animal

I eat insects, fruits, fish or even blood.
I live in caves.
I have extremely sharp teeth.
I can fly.
I am nocturnal.
I can see in the dark.
What am I?

Answer: A bat.

Lacey Wilkinson (6)
North Ormesby Primary Academy, Middlesbrough

A Woodland Animal

I have long ears.
I am a herbivore.
I have fluff all over me.
I have a white mouth.
I live in a cage or in the wild.
I live in burrows.
What am I?

Answer: A rabbit.

Zahra Baig (6)
North Ormesby Primary Academy, Middlesbrough

A Woodland Animal

I have long ears.
I am a herbivore.
I make holes which are called burrows.
I can be a pet or live in the wild.
Female ones are called does.
What am I?

Answer: A rabbit.

Viola D'Arcangelo (7)

North Ormesby Primary Academy, Middlesbrough

A Woodland Animal

I am nocturnal.
I have wings.
I have feathers to keep me warm.
I am a bird.
I live in a tree.
I have a tight grip.
What am I?

Answer: An owl.

Layten Spencer (7)
North Ormesby Primary Academy, Middlesbrough

A Woodland Animal

I have red fur.
I have sharp teeth.
I have sharp claws.
I am a carnivore.
I am nocturnal.
I have a long nose.
What am I?

Answer: A fox.

Jack Pattison (7)

North Ormesby Primary Academy, Middlesbrough

A Woodland Animal

I have a red tummy.
I lay eggs.
I sleep at night.
I eat worms.
I can fly.
I live in a tree.
What am I?

Answer: A robin.

Laavanya Paramalingam (6)
North Ormesby Primary Academy, Middlesbrough

A Woodland Animal

I am nocturnal.
I have talons to help me catch my prey.
I live in woodland.
I can't move my eyes.
What am I?

Answer: An owl.

Tharun Ahilan (6)
North Ormesby Primary Academy, Middlesbrough

What Am I?

I live in the southeastern parts of Australia including Tasmania.
I like to crawl on my tummy and my feet.
I also live in bushy woodlands.
I have a blue tongue.
I have little eyes.
I have little claws.
What am I?

Answer: A blue-tongued lizard.

Ava Tyas (7)

Pollington-Balne CE Primary School & Preschool, Pollington

What Am I?

I make a scurrying sound.
I like to slither around tall trees in
the forest.
I eat little, tiny green bugs.
I am black as the night with a red belly.
I live inside the tall trees in the jungle.
What am I?

Answer: A red-bellied black snake.

Lily May Tomlison (7)
Pollington-Balne CE Primary School & Preschool,
Pollington

What Am I?

I like to crawl through the deepest green grass.
I live in a wide open desert.
I can eat juicy slimy snails and vegetables.
I am a long black thing with a blue tongue.
I am brilliant at using my tongue.
What am I?

Answer: A blue-tongued lizard.

Samuel John Kealey (7)

Pollington-Balne CE Primary School & Preschool, Pollington

What Am I?

I stick my long tongue in and out.
I am slippery like a snake.
I eat meat that is tasty and delicious.
I eat flowers and juicy grass.
My home is in a tree.
My home needs to be warm.
What am I?

Answer: A blue-tongued lizard.

George Beard (6)
Pollington-Balne CE Primary School & Preschool,
Pollington

What Am I?

I like to scamper with my friends and dig for food.
I live in a hot desert together as a big group.
I look furry, soft and cuddly.
I like to eat meat, bugs and scrumptious fruit.
What am I?

Answer: A meerkat.

Zoë Mae (6)
Pollington-Balne CE Primary School & Preschool, Pollington

What Am I?

I look like a red-bellied and half black creature.
I creep up and bite
I have got eyes and a mouth but you cannot see them.
I like to eat frogs and baby mammals.
What am I?

Answer: A red-bellied black snake.

Darcey Bell (6)
Pollington-Balne CE Primary School & Preschool, Pollington

What Am I?

I live in a forest.
I have scaly skin.
I like to slither up the tree.
I like to eat fat frogs.
I have a red belly and a black body.
What am I?

Answer: A red-bellied black snake.

Finlay Laycock-Brown (6)

Pollington-Balne CE Primary School & Preschool,
Pollington

What Am I?

I am very fluffy and I'm very cute.
I like to roam around in the desert.
I like to eat meat and slimy lizards.
I live in a dusty, dirty desert.
What am I?

Answer: A meerkat.

Zachary Bamforth (7)
Pollington-Balne CE Primary School & Preschool,
Pollington

What Am I?

I live in the rainforest.
I like to eat tasty grass and crunchy slugs.
I like to run through the long grass.
I have a blue tongue.
What am I?

Answer: A blue-tongued lizard.

Edward Arthur Lacy (6)
Pollington-Balne CE Primary School & Preschool, Pollington

What Am I?

I look like a horrid disgusting worm.
I eat yummy beetles.
I like to slither on bumpy rocks.
I look like a scaly snake.
What am I?

Answer: A blue-tongued lizard.

Chance Downs (7)
Pollington-Balne CE Primary School & Preschool,
Pollington

What Am I?

I have a smooth furry body.
I live in a harsh desert.
I have little black sharp claws.
I am very good at listening for food.
What am I?

Answer: A meerkat.

Kian Biddle (7)
Pollington-Balne CE Primary School & Preschool, Pollington

What Am I?

I hang onto trees.
I have big round ears.
I live in a big tree.
I eat crunchy leaves.
I am grey and furry.
What am I?

Answer: A koala bear.

Lacey Mae Brook (5)

Pollington-Balne CE Primary School & Preschool,
Pollington

What Am I?

I have very furry ears.
I climb up trees all of the time.
I have a pointed nose.
I live in the treetops.
What am I?

Answer: A koala bear.

Annabel Bamforth (5)
Pollington-Balne CE Primary School & Preschool,
Pollington

What Am I?

I am slimy and chubby.
I live underwater.
I eat green seaweed.
I like to scare fish.
What am I?

Answer: A blobfish.

Grace Isabelle Davison (6)

Pollington-Balne CE Primary School & Preschool,
Pollington

What Am I?

I have slime on my body.
I am pink.
I eat crabs in the sea.
I live in the sea.
What am I?

Answer: A blobfish.

Penny Scofyald (6)
Pollington-Balne CE Primary School & Preschool,
Pollington

This Guy's Fun Riddle

I'm alive, but not animal or plant.
Some you can eat, some you can't.
I have gills but cannot swim.
I grow where it is dim.
Sometimes deadly, sometimes nice.
Sometimes nibbled by mice.
A room with no window or door,
I grow on the forest floor.
What am I?

Answer: A mushroom.

Inigo Blake-James (7)
St Mary & St Joseph RC (VA) Primary School,
Pocklington

Glowing And Growing

I make lots of smoke.
I'm in a grate.
I'm extremely hot.
You put coal, paper and wood on me
to burn.
I've a mantle.
I keep the house warm.
I'm red, orange and yellow.
What am I?

Answer: A fire.

Henry McLaughlin (6)
St Mary & St Joseph RC (VA) Primary School,
Pocklington

A Bird That Lived In Mauritius

I have a yellow beak.
I have brownish, greyish, blackish feathers.
I have yellow feet.
I have wings but I can't fly.
I lived alongside humans.
I am an egg layer.
I am extinct.
What am I?

Answer: A dodo.

William Roelofs (6)
St Mary & St Joseph RC (VA) Primary School, Pocklington

Hopping Hopper

I eat grass.
I am a vegetarian.
I have powerful legs.
I can jump very high.
Farmers don't like me very much.
I am cute in a cartoon.
I am quite small.
What am I?

Answer: A grasshopper.

Jessica Baines (7)

St Mary & St Joseph RC (VA) Primary School,
Pocklington

Cheeky, Cheeky

I have wings.
I have hair.
I have eyes.
I like apples.
I have four legs.
I have ears.
I have a horn.
I have rainbow hair.
I have white fluffy hair.
What am I?

Answer: A unicorn.

Natalie Leia Coldbeck (6)
St Mary & St Joseph RC (VA) Primary School,
Pocklington

Cutie

I have furry, long ears.
I have a cute short tail.
I twitch my cute nose.
I love carrots for lunch.
I jump very high.
I am cute and cuddly.
What am I?

Answer: A bunny.

Faith Cherry Patricia Bird (6)
St Mary & St Joseph RC (VA) Primary School,
Pocklington

I Am Good At Running And Scoring

I have bright football boots.
I have a T-shirt that is dark blue and light blue.
I have long socks.
I have muddy knees.
I have gloves.
What am I?

Answer: A footballer.

Aaron Wilce (7)

St Mary & St Joseph RC (VA) Primary School, Pocklington

Up And Down

You climb me.
You wrap me around things.
You swing me.
You play with me.
I come in many shapes and sizes.
Lots of people use me.
What am I?

Answer: Rope.

Max Anthony Burton (7)
St Mary & St Joseph RC (VA) Primary School,
Pocklington

A Furry Friend

I come in different colours.
You hug me.
I have a cute nose.
I love picnics.
I hate baths.
I help you go to sleep.
What am I?

Answer: A teddy bear.

Hannah Foster (6)
St Mary & St Joseph RC (VA) Primary School,
Pocklington

Fly In The Sky

It has a tail.
It is pretty.
It has wings.
It has a horn.
It has magic.
It loves rainbows.
It has hair
What is it?

Answer: A unicorn.

Martha Haselock (6)
St Mary & St Joseph RC (VA) Primary School,
Pocklington

Jumpy Pet

I have sharp teeth.
I have four legs.
I have ears.
I have claws on each paw.
I have a tail.
I have a mouth.
What am I?

Answer: A dog.

Dale Luke Patrick Feehan (6)
St Mary & St Joseph RC (VA) Primary School,
Pocklington

Beautiful

It flies around in the jungle.
It is very pretty.
It only likes warm weather.
It used to be a caterpillar.
What is it?

Answer: A butterfly.

Lois Hollingsworth (5)
St Mary & St Joseph RC (VA) Primary School,
Pocklington

Crazy Lily

I have ears.
I have black and white fur.
I have sharp teeth.
I have a tail.
I can bite.
I can lick.
What am I?

Answer: A dog.

Pamella Kapostina (6)
St Mary & St Joseph RC (VA) Primary School,
Pocklington

A Flying Friend

It has beautiful colours.
It flies.
It sits on flowers.
It comes from a caterpillar.
What is it?

Answer: A butterfly.

Amy Foster (6)

St Mary & St Joseph RC (VA) Primary School,
Pocklington

Bob

You ride me in a war.
My grandad used me.
I eat straw.
What am I?

Answer: A war horse.

Cadan Barnes (6)
St Mary & St Joseph RC (VA) Primary School,
Pocklington

Jumpy Jessy

I have fluffy fur.
I have a wet nose.
I have four legs.
What am I?

Answer: A dog.

Lucy Scott (7)
St Mary & St Joseph RC (VA) Primary School,
Pocklington

What A Shot

I use my feet.
I sprint a lot.
I kick a ball.
What am I?

Answer: A footballer.

Stanley Pardoe (7)

St Mary & St Joseph RC (VA) Primary School,
Pocklington

Happy Feet

It is cold and icy where we live.
So we have to cuddle tight.
We have wings but we cannot fly.
So we cannot go to a great height.
My flippers help me swim, which is what I love the most.
I live where you send letters to Santa in the post.
What am I?

Answer: A penguin.

Miley Isabell Kirby (6)
Thorngumbald Primary School, Thorngumbald

Super Bright

I come out at night without being called.
I am lost in the day without being stolen.
You can't touch me, but if you are lucky.
You might catch me shooting.
I am very bright.
But not a light.
What am I?

Answer: A star.

Holly Ellington-Runkee (7)
Thorngumbald Primary School, Thorngumbald

What Am I?

I'm round but not a wheel.
I'm sticky but not glue.
I'm see-through and very, very long.
I'm a snail but have no shell.
I come in many sizes.
I help on the happiest days.
What am I?

Answer: Sellotape.

Erica-Kay Watson (6)
Thorngumbald Primary School, Thorngumbald

Dim

I come out at night.
Some people are scared of me.
Some animals come out when I'm here.
When you switch the light on, I'm gone!
I cannot be touched.
In the morning I disappear.
What am I?

Answer: Darkness.

Demi Leonard (6)
Thorngumbald Primary School, Thorngumbald

Curly

I am very clean.
I am intelligent.
I come in different colours.
I live on a farm.
You can eat me.
I get big and fat.
I have a snout.
I have four trotters.
What am I?

Answer: A pig.

Rosie Cox (5)
Thorngumbald Primary School, Thorngumbald

The Master

I am small.
I am green.
I have got pointy ears.
My best friend is Luke.
I am extremely wise.
I live in a hut.
I am master of the Jedi
Who am I?

Answer: Yoda.

Jack Marks (7)
Thorngumbald Primary School, Thorngumbald

Splish Splash

I'm healthy and clean.
Sometimes I am green.
I come out of a tap.
I come from the sky.
I come out of your eyes when you cry.
What am I?

Answer: Water.

Imogen Ward (6)
Thorngumbald Primary School, Thorngumbald

Lightning

I am black and yellow.
I am very fast.
I hunt for my prey.
I have a tail.
I live in the savannah.
I have spots.
What am I?

Answer: A cheetah.

Charlotte Finer (6)
Thorngumbald Primary School, Thorngumbald

Mighty King

I am the king of the class
The hairiest of them all.
My arms are the length of a car
I grow enormously tall.
I am the boss of my kingdom
I am as strong as a house.
But my legs aren't as strong
Even though they could crush a mouse.
What am I?

Answer: A gorilla.

Jack McKenzie Fletcher (6)
Woodmansey Primary School, Woodmansey

The Fierce Roar

I have big whiskers.
I love hunting.
I make loud noises.
I have a long tail with a fluffy end.
I love sleeping.
I feel soft.
I can kill you.
I am very fierce.
What am I?

Answer: A lion.

Annie Hall (5)
Woodmansey Primary School, Woodmansey

Green Apple

I am small and I like to wiggle,
I climb stalks so I don't get stood on.
I like to eat apples,
Soon I will turn into a butterfly.
What am I?

Answer: A caterpillar.

Rubie Ellen Cook (7)
Woodmansey Primary School, Woodmansey

Flyer Fangs

I fly at night.
I give people a fright.
I have fangs.
I live somewhere where you hear bangs.
I am dark.
I may fly through the park
What am I?

Answer: A bat.

Darcy Bishop (7)
Woodmansey Primary School, Woodmansey

Scary And Stripy

Watch me pounce.
See me bounce.
Hear me roar and growl.
Fear me as I prowl.
Count my stripes.
I'm scary, yikes!
What am I?

Answer: A tiger.

Isaac John Clapham Walker (6)
Woodmansey Primary School, Woodmansey

Wriggle, Wriggle

I am wriggly.
I am green.
I eat leaves.
I rest and hatch.
Then I am beautiful.
I fly away.
What am I?

Answer: A butterfly.

James Wilbor (7)
Woodmansey Primary School, Woodmansey

Soft And Warm

I have four legs.
I have two ears.
I live on a farm.
I come in different colours.
I have a mane.
What am I?

Answer: A horse.

Imogen Eden Ward (7)
Woodmansey Primary School, Woodmansey

A Growling Friend

I can howl.
I sleep in the day.
I stay awake in the night.
I eat rabbits.
I live in the woods.
What am I?

Answer: Wolf.

Alex Fratson (5)
Woodmansey Primary School, Woodmansey